Eudora Space Kid:
The Great Engine Room Takeover

Table of Contents

First paperback edition 2021

Illustration and book design by Talitha Shipman

ISBN 978-1-7366774-0-7 (paperback)
ISBN 978-1-7366774-1-4 (ebook)

www.eudoraspacekid.com

Dedicated to my two wonderful ribbon children
who love Eudora's stories even more than I do.
And sorry to my wife for forgetting to do the laundry.
But I was in the middle of writing Chapter Eight.

Book One
The Great Engine Room Takeover

By
David Horn

Illustrated by
Talitha Shipman

Designation: Athena
Class: AstroLiner
Weapons: Lots
Swimming pools: 5

Chapter One
Plasma Cannons 101

"**O**uch!" Lootenant (I'm not sure how to spell it, but this looks right) Londo screamed as he bent down to look at his toe, which I had just stepped on. He is the AstroLiner *Athena*'s biggest, strongest officer. More than big, he's not even human.

Londo is actually a Qlaxon from a scary planet called Qlaxonia. Normally he wouldn't even notice if third grader Eudora Jenkins, the all-around most awesome girl on the *Athena*, stepped on his foot. But I really needed Londo to look away from the weapons console he was standing over.

Bridge of the *Athena*

So I created a distraction. You see, I needed to get to the plasma cannon controls.

We live on the *Athena*, and my third-grade class was on a tour of the spaceship's bridge. We had won the tour in a school-wide essay contest about the important traits, like honesty and respect, of an AstroFleet officer. I tried to get them to add *fun* as a trait, but Miss Allison, our teacher, said, "There is absolutely no way under the stars I would do that." We won, so maybe she was right.

Anyway, a tour of the bridge is very rare. Some kids never get to see the bridge. Oh, the bridge is on Deck 36, where all the senior officers, including the captain, control the ship and fight space battles. Captain Jax *hates* having kids on his bridge, probably because he's scared of things like the exact plan I had in mind since we won the contest. If a kid ever happened to walk onto the bridge, Captain Jax would yell, "Get that kid off my bridge!" And then Lootenant Londo would take the kid's arm and walk them off the bridge. I know this is true because I've tried. Many times.

And while Captain Jax looks like a big Santa Claus, except with curly red hair on his head and beard, his whole body shakes when he yells. It looks like his body is yelling at the same time as his mouth.

But still, Captain Jax just doesn't realize how I absolutely need and cannot live without actually firing the *Athena*'s plasma cannons. Ever since we won the contest, I have been dreaming about it. What could possibly be more exciting than firing some of the most awesome space weapons in all of AstroFleet? I even told my best friend, Arnold, about it. But he just said, "Eudora, are you going to do one of your stupid plans again?"

So my cunning (no, Arnold, not stupid) plan was to build a hypersonic shocking device small enough to fit in my shoe. It would shock Lootenant Londo's toes when I stepped on the big Qlaxon's foot. He would then have to look down and away from the console. And as you can see, it worked like a charm. But really, my inventions usually do.

I love science, math, and engineering. Engineering is basically building fun things using math and science, so it's perfect for me. And I usually build things so I can have more fun. One day I want to be a chief engineer of an AstroLiner, though I would settle for captain. Miss Allison already calls me Chief Eudora during our science classes.

Anyway, as soon as Londo bent down, I quickly found the computer buttons I needed to press.

As part of my plan, I had learned the *Athena*'s weapons systems. So I quickly found my target and pressed down on the button that said "Fire."

Boom!

The *Athena* rattled, and all the senior officers, who were looking at Lootenant Londo cringe in pain, quickly turned to look at the viewport. The viewport is the screen at the front of the bridge that looks out into space. A purple stream of plasma was shooting from the *Athena*'s cannons to a nearby asteroid. The asteroid exploded.

"Yes!" I screamed and threw my arms in the air in celebration.

Unfortunately, Captain Jax exploded, too.

"Eudora!" the captain—and his belly—yelled.

"To the brig, now!"

Chapter Two
To the Brig

Captain Jax didn't think it was so amazing that a third-grade girl knew so much about AstroLiner operations that she could fire plasma cannons. Grown-ups don't like it when us kids know how to do adult things. But can't Captain Jax see that I can help him in a battle against evil aliens? Anyway, I got put in the brig, which is basically AstroLiner jail for AstroFleet officers and anyone else on board who gets caught being naughty.

"They put you in jail? A third grader?" you ask (even if you didn't, you probably should have). Yes, can you believe they put me in jail? But there is a story behind that, too.

You see, my mom, Wilma Jenkins, is a lootenant commander in AstroFleet with the important job of running the brig on this ship. So when I say Captain Jax put me in the brig, he basically sent me to my mom. She's there almost all the time. In fact, the only place she can watch me during the day is from the brig. Well, she's supposed to be watching. But I always just see her reading books with kissing on the cover. Ew!

And officers in AstroFleet work a lot, so I even celebrated my fifth birthday from the brig while my mom worked. Can you believe it? Even poor Ensign Matthews sang "Happy Birthday" to me from her holding cell in the brig. She was there for starting a food fight in Cafeteria 2. By the way, do not eat at Cafeteria 2. I hear it gets wild in there.

And the holding cells (the little rooms where they put you) are not so bad. They each come with a comfy bench and have see-through doors. But my mom never closes my

door. And the bench is even comfier than the bed in my room.

"You did what to who, Eudora?" my mom asked me as Lootenant Londo walked me into the brig. He was still walking funny.

"Um. . . I kind of stepped on his toe," I said softly while pointing my thumb at the big alien Qlaxon, who was looking angrily at me.

"And now he's limping?" my mom asked. She was very surprised.

"Grrr," Lootenant Londo growled.

"But he's. . . ," my mom said, pointing really high with her finger at him. "And you're. . ."She pointed really low at me.

"Grrr," Lootenant Londo growled a little louder. "Ask her about the weapons," he said in his deep voice.

"Weapons! You gave a third grader weapons?"

My mom was angry. She took her furry paw and started rubbing my head. I love when she does that. She has the softest fur of any mom I know! You see, she's from the lovable dog-like species named Pox from the planet Pox, which is a member of the Planetary Republic along with Earth.

My mom looks a little like a beautiful gray wolf standing up straight, with amazingly soft gray fur over her entire body. She is a really great snuggler with all that soft fur. I love when her soft, fuzzy paws wrap around me. But don't tell her I said that!

"Mr. Londo, I am shocked and dismayed to find this out. I'll be reporting this to Vice Captain Ying," my mom continued.

Way to go, Mom! You see, Vice Captain Stella Ying is the boss of all the other senior officers, including Londo. All the officers on board agree that she is the toughest officer on the ship, even though she is a very small lady with short black hair. She's half the size of Lootenant Londo.

One time Lootenant Londo brought her chocolate instead of vanilla ice cream during a senior officer ice cream social. She was so angry she made him clean up Cafeteria 2 for a whole month. After every meal! With only a spoon!

And even though Captain Jax is her boss, he is probably scared of her, too.

"Um...," Londo said and then walked out of the brig, clearly scared of Vice Captain Ying.

"Mom," I said softly. "It was kind of my fault." I paused to see what she would say, but she stayed quiet and looked closer at me. "We were on our bridge tour, and..." I paused again.

"I really liked your essay," she said. "You know, on honesty. Honesty is very important."

She knew I had done something wrong,

but she had still defended me in front of Lootenant Londo.

"Yes, I'm trying, Mom. Well, I kind of pressed the 'Fire' button on the plasma cannons."

"Eudora Lucille Jenkins! Tell me you did not destroy a ship!"

"Asteroid, Mother," I said quietly.

"To the cells, now!" she yelled and led me to a holding cell where I sat down on a bench.

"Make sure you do your homework. If you finish in time, I'll let you out to see your father play in the Ping-Pong tournament tonight," she said, smiling again.

Chapter Three
My Space Family

Chief Galactic
Spelling Bee Planner
MOLLY JENKINS

My mom always knows how to make me feel better. I love watching my father win the ship-wide Ping-Pong tournament every year.

You see, my father, Max Jenkins, is from an octopus-like species from the planet Pow, which is also a member of the Planetary Republic. He stands like a human, but has an octopus head instead of a human head. His feet look more like octopus arms shaped like feet, and he has more octopus arms on his upper body. He can definitely help my mom and me get pickle jars open! And he wins the *Athena*'s annual Ping-Pong tournament every single year. I couldn't wait to watch him that night.

So, as you can see, I'm actually a human girl adopted by what you might call aliens. And you thought your parents were weird. But I love them, and they care about me a lot. They adopted both me and my older, super-boring know-it-all sister, Molly, when we were very little.

Molly is super boring because her main goal in life is to have grown-ups say, "Good job, Molly." This means she can never have any fun because when you are having fun, grown-ups usually say different things like, "Put that down!" or "Stop putting that tarantula in your sister's oatmeal!" But I'm glad I have her because I can tell she does care about me, just like my mom.

We actually both want to be officers in AstroFleet in the future, but I think AstroFleet would give her a boring job like Chief Galactic Spelling Bee Planner, or Commander of Finally Finding Out if There Are Actually More Grains of Sand Than Stars. She would like the sand thing!

And when I'm not in the brig, I live with my family in Cabin 7 on Deck 22. Luckily, Molly and I have our own rooms. But she got the bigger room with the comfier bed.

By the way, I wasn't the only person in a brig holding cell that afternoon. You wouldn't think grown-ups on the most important ship in the Planetary Republic would need a brig, but they do. Why, just the other day, my mom told me about what Commander Wilson did. She lost a game of Spit (an ancient Earth card game of speed) to a lootenant (in Cafeteria 2, by the way) and actually spit on her! She had to go to the brig for a time-out.

Things like that happen all the time. Grown-ups think they're so great, but us space kids know what really happens on the *Athena*.

Oh my, I forgot to tell you about the *Athena*!

The AstroLiner *Athena* is AstroFleet's flagship. AstroFleet is the science and defense force for the Planetary Republic. We are usually out exploring some strange new planet or star and doing science experiments. Once we even discovered a new planet with friendly aliens. My parents took me to a type of shopping mall there, but they only bought me socks. "Spaceships are cold, so you need warm socks," my mom always says.

When I'm captain one day, I'm going to create Flip-Flop Fridays, and all the officers will have to wear flip-flops. Maybe it will be so popular they'll do it across the entire Republic!

Oh yeah, I forgot to mention that the Planetary Republic is a group of twenty planets that have agreed to work together to make the galaxy a better place for all living things—humans, aliens, robots, turtles... really anything except for rocks because they aren't living. But we still care about rocks.

Being the flagship in AstroFleet means that our ship is the biggest in the fleet. It has the most people, the biggest engines, and the most weapons, like my favorite plasma cannons. We even have two cafeterias! But please do not go to Cafeteria 2; you may get wet (I hear there are lots of food fights in there).

We also have a lot of people who live on the *Athena*. Many people are AstroFleet officers, but there are a lot of people who are not, like my teacher, Miss Allison, and, of course, us space kids. That's what the grown-ups call us kids who grow up on spaceships and don't have backyards and don't ride school buses like you land kids.

I would do anything to be an officer in AstroFleet, exploring and saving the universe from the evil Qlaxons. (Boo! When you hear *Qlaxons* you're supposed to say boo loudly. They are the meanest aliens out there, and you want to annoy them by saying boo. They have excellent hearing, so they may actually hear you! Go ahead, try it!). The Qlaxons are from the planet Qlaxonia, which isn't a member of the Republic because it wants all the other planets in the galaxy for itself. Miss Allison would say that is not the way to behave with friends.

And while Qlaxonia is not in the Planetary Republic, there are a few Qlaxons who have left Qlaxonia to join the Republic over the years. That is how Londo ended up in AstroFleet. I heard that Londo's parents left Qlaxonia to join the Republic when Londo was only a baby. I can't imagine how they found diapers big enough for a baby Qlaxon, but I'm scared to ask him! You can, though!

Qlaxons look like those lions from Earth that I've seen in books and videos, except they can stand up and talk. Like lions, they have yellow catlike faces, golden fur, and big golden manes. They are usually dressed in round metal uniforms that make them look like lions stuck in soda cans. That's even scarier because if they really were stuck in soda cans, then they would be even madder!

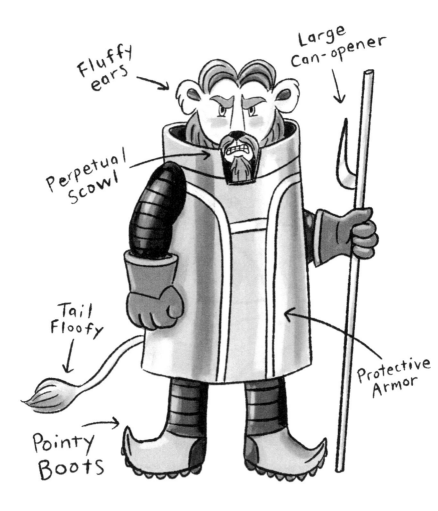

Qlaxon Warrior

Chapter Four
Engine Room 101

One day a few weeks after the toe incident, I had an even better idea than firing the plasma cannons.

It all started while I was at school on Deck 12. The school has a big circular main lobby with doors all around it that open to the different classrooms. It is usually one classroom per grade. This would be okay, but it means that I see Molly at school every single day, no matter what, especially during lunch. She's in eighth grade, so she's only a few doors down from me. If we were land kids, I think we would be in different buildings, and she could never tell my parents how I threw

my applesauce at that naughty boy, Sammy Roper. She sometimes even asks Miss Allison for a list of all my homework assignments so she can check up on me! Sometimes you land kids are lucky.

Anyway, we were in the middle of our science period, which is one of my favorite times of the day. But the lesson that day got me really thinking, which Arnold always says can be dangerous. Miss Allison kept talking about hyperdrive, which is what our ship uses to travel faster than the speed of light. She said how no ship in AstroFleet has ever gone faster than 10 on the HyperDrive-O-Meter. Then Miss Allison said, "Maybe one day our Chief Eudora can get a ship faster than 10. I'm pretty sure she'll try."

One day? How about today? Can I improve the engines? Could I somehow make the *Athena* break all known space speed records? It was worth a shot! And if I could make the *Athena* go faster than ever before, maybe Captain Jax would promote me to ensign (the first level for officers in AstroFleet). Then I could skip the rest of elementary school and all of middle school. Why not just go straight to chief engineer? If I could break space speed records, he would have to do that. You agree with me, right?

I started sketching and writing a lot of engine ideas. Maybe if I adjust the flax transistor and bypass the berry conduit . . .

Once I started thinking, I couldn't stop. I suddenly had pages of ideas. But first I had to figure out a way to get into the *Athena*'s engine room to actually try my ideas out. They wouldn't just let little Eudora Jenkins walk into the engine room and start working on a computer console. This was tricky.

Older kids, including us third graders, are usually dismissed from school on our own without any parents there to ask us if we forgot anything. Sometimes I have an after-school activity. On Mondays I have dance with Vice Captain Stella Ying (how do you think I first learned that step-on-the-toe move?). On Wednesdays I have heavy metal electric-rock-god guitar class with Mr. Bertucci (or, as he calls it, Guitar Lessons for Beginners, Class 1B). All the other days I get to do whatever I want after school. Well, after homework of course.

This day after school I decided that I would go to the engine room. The engine room is on Decks 1 through 4. Normally there is never any reason for kids to be on Decks 1 through 4. So I had to think of something. Hmmm . . . my pet drago named Bologna escaped, and I'm looking for her?

By the way, I'm the one who named our drago. Well, kind of. When my parents told us we were getting a drago, I screamed boloney as if they were lying to me. And the name stuck, but my parents said to spell it the fancy way, like the lunch meat, because our drago is a "lady." Oh, and we feed her bologna for lunch, too.

I can't believe I forgot. You don't know what a drago is, do you? Imagine a creature that is a mix between a bunny and a dragon. It looks like a dragon, is about the size of a

bunny, and has fuzzy fur. Instead of breathing fire, it breathes love at everyone it meets. You get some love! You get some love! And you get some love!

Chapter Five
The Plan

Normally finding a loose pet on the *Athena* would be easy. The science department has scanners that can find living things. But dragos have a special chemical in their fur that disrupts all scanners. You can imagine how many lost dragos there are all over the *Athena*! So I decided that I would pretend I'm looking for Bologna.

After school let out, Molly stopped me and said, "I'm going to do my homework back at the cabin. Want to come? I'll let you play with some of my math problems."

I usually love when Molly lets me play with

her homework problems (it might be the one thing we have in common), but this was not the day for that.

"Um. . . I would love to, but I have somewhere to be," I said, trying to get rid of her.

"What do you have? Dance is on Mondays, and guitar is on Wednesdays. You don't have anything today," she said suspiciously.

"Um. . . It probably would be better to not start all my sentences with *um*, doh!" Oops, I said that all out loud!

Now Molly looked suspicious and really confused. This was not going well.

"Hiya, Eudora!" Arnold said. He came out of the school and bounced toward us. Arnold is in my class and is about my size. We are two of the smaller kids in our class. He has wavy blond hair that he wears kind of long, so his hair was bouncing, too. "Miss Allison just gave me an A on my Jamestown Settlement essay. She wants me to read it out loud at the school speech competition in a few weeks."

"Let's go practice, Arnold," I said as I grabbed his arm and yanked him, and me, out of there.

"Ouch! What did you do that for?" Arnold said, looking like I hurt his arm and his feelings.

"I needed to get away from Molly. I have something I have to do. See you later," I said

and started to walk off, still carrying my school backpack.

"But I thought you were going to help me," he cried.

I felt kind of bad, but one good thing about Arnold is that he is a patient and understanding friend. He must have learned that from having such a tough, strong Qlaxon as a father.

"Wait, Arnold is an evil Qlaxon?" you must be asking yourself. No, but our chief of security, Lootenant Londo, is his stepdad. You see, him and his mother, Dolores, are human. She works in a nail salon on the *Athena*. (I told you we had the most of everything.) She met and married Lootenant Londo years ago when he was first stationed here. Whamo, instant Qlaxon dad.

Arnold once told me how his Qlaxon grandparents still own a shoe store on Earth in some place called Noo Joyzee. He visits them sometimes and always comes back with really cool new sneakers. I have to find a way to get to Noo Joyzee sometime. My parents always just get me the smaller version of whatever my sister Molly picks out. And she usually picks just plain white. Super boring! Not like Noo Joyzee!

"I will help you after you recite it in the mirror for a few hours," I replied to Arnold confidently. "I need something to work with, Arnold. You need to prepare the ingredients before I can bake the cake," I continued as I pretended to be mixing a bowl of cake batter with my hands. "See you later!"

And then I ran off with all my sketches and calculations and headed to the AstroTram, which is an elevator on the *Athena*. It can go up, down, left, and right. The AstroTram would take me near the main entrance of the engine room on Deck 1.

I got off the tram car, and the hallway on Deck 1 was crowded with officers shuffling about. Not shuffling like dancing, just milling. But not milling like farming. . . Oh, fine. They were just walking around. I had to immediately implement my plan.

"Bologna!" I yelled as I started walking down Deck 1. "Bologna!"

Usually officers are busy and distracted, so they don't pay me too much attention, but of course this one time, Ensign Ramirez came over.

"Hi, little girl," she said. "Are you looking for the cafeteria?"

Ensign is the lowest rank in AstroFleet, so she was younger than the other officers. Ensigns usually have recently graduated from Astro University, the college for future AstroFleet officers. She was a plain-looking lady with long brown hair.

"No, Ensign Ramirez. I am not looking for a sandwich," I said, annoyed, "My pet drago, Bologna, is missing, and I am looking for her."

I make it a point to know most of the officers on the *Athena*, since I will be serving with them in AstroFleet one day. Usually they know who I am because, well, because of things like the toe incident. But apparently Ensign Ramirez didn't know who I was. This was not a time to fix that.

"Oh, let me help," she said. And before I could say no, she was yelling, "Bologna! Bologna!" while walking in a circle around the hall near us. This was not the type of help I wanted. But very soon she said, "Now I'm hungry for lunch," and she stopped what she was doing and walked off down the hallway. What kind of help was that, Ensign Ramirez? But she had left, so my plan was a success so far.

As I continued down the hallway, I occasionally yelled, "Bologna! Bologna!" Ensign Ramirez was not the only officer who heard me and was reminded of lunch. I heard other officers start to ask each other about lunch.

"Hey, it's getting close to mealtime," one officer said to no one in particular.

"Anyone see the Cafeteria 1 menu today?" another officer asked the group he was walking down the hallway with.

This gave me another idea!

The hallway was now empty, so I quickly made my way to the main entrance of the engine room. I found a computer control panel on the wall near the entrance. I took a screwdriver out of my backpack and was able to take the cover off the panel.

I also keep a lot of electronics in my bag because you never know when you'll have to build something fun. I took out a microphone and connected it to the control panel. With the microphone I could control the public address system in the engine room. You may call the public address system an intercom, loudspeaker, or just the PA system.

Officers and non-officers can access the PA system from any computer console. But officers also get special AstroFleet-issued watches that have tiny speakers and microphones inside. The officers even get a choice of ten colors, or one with a picture of some ancient Earth mouse on it named Mookie! But us kids don't get these. Totally not fair!

With access to the PA system, I then started carrying out my idea. I used my lowest, most grown-up voice and said, "Attention engine room. Attention engine room. Please head to Cafeteria 2 immediately for ice cream and cake to celebrate Captain Jax's birthday."

Immediately, the engine room door opened, and all the engineers ran out cheering, "Ice cream! Cake! Ice cream! Cake!"

Then I sneaked a peek inside the room. My plan worked! The engine room was empty, so I disconnected my microphone and quietly walked inside.

Chapter Six
Scene of the Crime

Wow, the engine room was big! The fusion chamber, where the ship's fuel was stored and used, was four stories tall with walkways circling it. Various computers lined the walls.

I had forgotten how huge it was. I was there on a Halloween field trip a few years ago. The engineers had decorated the engine room as a spooky walk for us kids. I'll always remember it because I "accidentally" dropped the pumpkin I had just picked into the fusion chamber. I told everyone it was an accident, but I really just wanted to see what would happen.

It wasn't good. They had to stop the engines, Chief Fraser was covered in pumpkin seeds, and the *Athena* was stuck in place for three days while they cleaned the chamber. They still talk about the great pumpkin surprise.

I found my way to one of the computers and got to work. I took my electropad from my backpack. An electropad is an electronic device that has all your binders, notebooks, and school books in one, so you can never say you lost your homework. You can't even lose your electropad because the *Athena*'s computer always knows where it is.

I pulled up the special engineering notes I had made on my electropad during class. Then I used the computer login I got from Ensign Bixby. She was an officer who had left the *Athena* a few months ago. Ensign Bixby had left her login information written down on a piece of paper by a computer in the brig. My mom had let her log in so she could check the baseball scores back on Earth.

Baseball is some ancient Earth game with a ball, big mittens, and a wooden club. It's very strange. It's also very strange that Ensign Bixby kept her login information written down. You're not supposed to do that.

Anyway, using her login I was able to access the screen I wanted on the engine room's computer, and I made a few of my special adjustments. All of a sudden I heard a loud bang. This was the same sound I had heard when my pumpkin fell into the chamber. Just like then, I could hear the engine turn off, and the ship stopped completely. Uh-oh!

Immediately I heard Captain Jax on the ship-wide PA system. "Chief Engineer Fraser," he said. "What's going on down there? What happened to my ship?"

A moment passed, and then I heard Chief

Fraser respond, "Captain, I don't know. We aren't even in the engine room. We are waiting for the ice cream and cake in Cafeteria 2 to celebrate your birthday. Why aren't you here? We're tired of waiting."

"Chief Fraser, I have no idea what you're talking about," yelled Captain Jax. "Now get back to the engine room and fix the *Athena*'s engines!"

I knew I had to hide fast, so I crawled behind a large computer station in a small room next to the main room. All the engineers shuffled back in looking sad. I heard them muttering to one another.

"What happened to the cake?"

"I can't believe there was no ice cream!"

"What kind of birthday party was that?"

I had to do something quick, so I patched into the engine room's PA system again using my microphone, and I said in a much quieter, but still grown-up voice, "Attention engine room. The party for Captain Jax was supposed to be a surprise. Of course he doesn't know about it. Please head back to Cafeteria 2. Wait there until further instructions. Do not mention this to Captain Jax or you will ruin the surprise. And, yes, there will still be cake and ice cream."

A sudden cheer erupted in the engine room. I even heard Chief Fraser say, "That makes sense now! I hope they have pistachio-flavored ice cream. It's my favorite. Let's go, everybody! Now! Now! Now!"

Once again, all the engineers left the engine room in a hurry.

Chapter Seven
And the Galaxy's New Record Goes To...

I had to get back to work. I put the microphone back into my bag and walked to a computer terminal in the main room. I quickly brought up the computer screen that I needed and tried the second page of my special engine adjustments.

This time, instead of a bang I heard a whoosh. The ship immediately took off really fast, and I could see the HyperDrive-O-Meter on the computer screen go up and up. The *Athena*'s top speed record was 10 on the HyperDrive-O-Meter. But now, the ship was already at 9 and getting faster! I might actually break the record!

The HyperDrive-O-Meter kept going up and was already at 9.9, which is almost 10. But 9.9 wouldn't get me any awards or promotions to chief engineer. So I made some additional adjustments from page three of my special engine adjustment notes. I waited a few seconds more, and then I heard another whoosh.

The whole ship shook, and I fell back on my rump. I cautiously looked up at the HyperDrive-O-Meter, and it said 10.5. I did it. I broke the record! That's half a point faster than any ship in AstroFleet has ever gone. I knew I could do it!

All of a sudden, I heard the ship-wide PA system crackle.

"Engine room!" said Captain Jax.

I was sure he would be super excited!

"What is going on down there?" Captain Jax yelled. "Now we're breaking speed

records? Explain!"

Chief Engineer Fraser spoke up. "Captain, I don't know what to say. I'm not supposed to talk about it, but we're not even in the engine room."

"What do you mean you're not supposed to talk about it? I'm the captain. Tell me now!"

"But, Captain, I can't. Please don't make me tell you. If you do, you'll be sorry!" Chief Fraser replied, sounding exasperated.

"I'm sorry now that you won't tell me! I order you to tell me!" Captain Jax responded, sounding equally exasperated.

"But, Captain. If I do, I'll ruin the... the...," Chief Fraser stammered.

"The what?"

Captain Jax was on the edge of his seat. I could tell from his voice. I could picture him on the bridge sitting stiffly in the captain's chair. I was standing stiffly at the computer console in the engine room, hearing Captain Jax's voice get madder and madder.

"You're supposed to be in Cafeteria 2," Chief Fraser said.

"And you're supposed to be in the engine room! Now tell me, why are we breaking speed records? I didn't order this or authorize any engine experiments. And, frankly, I don't like when the ship goes too fast. It upsets my tummy!" Captain Jax complained.

This was too much. I had to explain my heroic efforts before Captain Jax got even madder. So I found the PA button on the computer terminal I was at and spoke into the computer. "Uh. . . Captain. . . is this thing on?" I said nervously.

"Who is this? Is that Eudora?" Captain Jax asked.

I was excited again. He recognized my voice! He knew my name! But then I realized, maybe he just remembered me from firing the plasma cannons a few days ago.

"Eudora?" Chief Fraser said. "Were you the one talking about the surprise party on the PA system earlier? We have been waiting for ages here in Cafeteria 2 for the cake and ice cream."

"Surprise party? Is that why you're not in the engine room, Chief Fraser?" Captain Jax asked.

"Fellow officers," I interrupted. "It was I who broke the record."

"What?" Chief Fraser exclaimed.

"What?" Captain Jax exclaimed.

Chapter Eight
The Eudora Method

"**E**udora, shut down the engines and stay where you are," Captain Jax ordered. "Chief Fraser, meet me at the engine room."

Uh-oh. He didn't sound happy.

"But, Captain, they haven't served the cake and ice cream yet," Chief Fraser whined.

"There is no cake and ice cream. It's not my birthday! Eudora tricked you." Captain Jax really didn't sound happy.

"She didn't trick just me, Captain. She tricked the whole engineering department," Chief Fraser said, defending himself. "We're on our way."

I shut down the engines and waited in the engine room, feeling pretty awful that they didn't seem to appreciate the new, totally awesome HyperDrive-O-Meter speed record I had achieved.

I was surprised. The *Athena* would be the talk of the fleet. The crews of the *Artemis*, the *Aphrodite*, and even the *Hephaestus* would be extremely jealous.

Actually, the *Hephaestus* crew is always jealous of the other ships because no one can pronounce its name correctly. I hear the senior officers of all the other ships just call it the hot dog, which makes the crew of the *Hephaestus* really mad. But hot dog is easier to say than *Hephaestus*, and it is painted red and yellow like a hot dog with mustard.

The engine room doors opened. Captain Jax and Chief Fraser appeared with the rest of the engineers behind them.

"Eudora! Are you all right? Are you injured?"

Captain Jax exclaimed.

"I'm fine. Did you see, Captain? We reached 10.5 on the HyperDrive-O-Meter!"

"Yes, we saw. But that was extremely dangerous. You could have been hurt. You could have damaged the *Athena*. You could have been covered with pumpkin seeds again!" Captain Jax looked extremely angry.

"And you lied about the ice cream." Chief Fraser added, also looking angry.

The rest of the engineers let out a big, angry, "Yeah!"

Wow, amazingly awesome speed records sure make people angry around here!

"But I knew what I was doing. And it worked! See?" I said while I pointed at the HyperDrive-O-Meter. But I knew I was in trouble.

"You know what is coming, Eudora," Captain Jax said.

"Yes, I know," I said softly.

"Let's go see your mother," he said, also softly.

"The brig," I said sadly and even more softly. "But can you at least tell my mom about the speed record?" I begged a little less softly.

"Of course, we definitely will. I think the rest of the Planetary Republic will be excited to hear about the Eudora Method, at least after we figure out what you did," Captain Jax said as we left the engine room and headed down the hallway. "But you can't keep breaking the rules, Eudora. You'll never become an officer that way. That's not how officers behave."

"But I've seen other officers in the brig! Did you hear about Commander Wilson?" I blurted out as we boarded the AstroTram.

"Those were minor mistakes, Eudora," the captain said as the tram started to move. "Everyone makes mistakes. You can make mistakes and still be an officer in AstroFleet.

But there is a difference between those mistakes and recklessly risking yourself and the ship on purpose."

"I think I understand," I said.

Grown-ups love it when they think you understand the important things they say. I'll have enough time to think about it while I'm in the brig anyway.

I felt bad, but then I realized one thing, and this one thing I would definitely think about while in the brig. Captain Jax called my engine adjustments the Eudora Method.

The Eudora Method!

About the Author

Chief Galactic
Squirrel Wrangler
TRIXIE

Hi, my name is Trixie. I was asked to write about my human owner, Dada. Or as you know him, David Horn. Dada lives with my other owner, Mama. Mama and Dada have two daughters, who are my human littermates. They are so much fun and we play so many games together - like stinky dino, fennis and soccer ruffball. I just don't like it when Dada and my human littermates watch those science fiction shows on the big box in the living room. I'd rather watch squirrels.

We live in New Jersey. It is called the Squirrel State. Oh, I mean the Garden State. I do love New Jersey, though, because I love to eat gardens. Dada has very tasty flowers and shrubs. He doesn't garden as much as when I first met him, though. Do you think it's my fault? That's okay because now he has more time for me. Speaking of time, do you have a moment to rub my belly? Please?

About the Illustrator

Hi, my name is Indy. I am a tiny French Brittany puppy and I live with a family of humans consisting of a Mom, a Dad, and a small squealy thing called a child. I haven't been with my human family long, but I can already tell that the one named Talitha is very odd. She sits in front of a glowing box all day long and draws pictures of spaceships and fluffy dragon bunnies.

The humans also watch another glowing box featuring some sort of war in the stars and some sort of trek across the stars. I think they may be ALIENS! Should I call the authorities?

Galactic Squirrel
Wrangler In Training
INDY

We live in Indiana. It is a nice place filled with squirrles and bunnies and chipmunks. It is called the Hoosier State. I have no idea why. Most of the humans don't seem to know why either.

Acknowledgments

I want to give a huge thank you to Talitha for such amazing art and design. All the funny stuff in the pictures were her ideas!

I also want to thank my daughters for being so patient while waiting to finally hold a Eudora book in their hands. Eudora started as funny stories I would tell my daughters over dinner, and seeing her in print was as much a dream for them as for me.

And thanks to Heather, Susan, Ruth, Jessica, and Ashley for such great editing and encouragement. I wouldn't and couldn't have done this without you!

Finally, the biggest thanks goes to my wife, because turning Eudora into a real book was all her idea. And now she gets to listen to me talk about Eudora endlessly. Sorry! And thanks!

More cosmic adventures featuring Eudora are coming soon!

Visit www.eudoraspacekid.com to learn more about the series.

Psst...hey kids, if you liked this book, grab a pencil and paper and write a review. Then bother the closest grown-up you can find to post your review on their favorite online bookstore. I'd love to hear what you think!

Eudora's Word Search

Hi! It's Eudora! I'm great at math. But I could really use your help to find these words. If you can find all the words, I'll sneak you onto the bridge so you can fire the plasma cannons! But we may end up in the. . . oh, that's the first word. . .

BRIG	**JAX**	**STELLA**
PLASMA	**ASTROFLEET**	**PISTACHIO**
ATHENA	**ALLISON**	**HYPERDRIVE**

A	L	L	I	S	O	N	P	D	R	E
O	S	K	R	A	X	Z	H	Q	Q	V
Z	T	T	V	Y	T	E	N	Y	H	I
P	E	B	R	I	G	H	R	Y	F	R
V	L	B	A	O	H	C	E	Z	G	D
J	L	A	N	V	F	W	W	N	R	R
O	A	U	S	Y	G	L	P	B	A	E
S	U	X	O	M	Z	M	E	O	P	P
B	J	X	C	Y	A	E	I	E	S	Y
P	I	S	T	A	C	H	I	O	T	H

Turn the page for a
sneak peek of Eudora's
Next Adventure

Eudora Space Kid: The Lobster Tale

Chapter One
Looking for Fun in All the Small Places

"**A**rnold, hand me that screwdriver," I whispered.

It was a Saturday morning and my best friend, Arnold, and I had crawled inside the air vent on Deck 36, right near the bridge.

Whoever designed the AstroLiner *Athena* accidentally made the air vents in the hallways big enough so that third-grade kids could get inside them. And once you crawl far enough inside the correct air vent, you can find a special tunnel. If you crawl through that very special tunnel, you can access small rooms that have a lot of the ship's computers. The computers are like the guts of the ship. I like to call these rooms gut rooms. I just love computer guts.

You see, my name is Eudora Jenkins, and while I'm only in the third grade, I'm a whiz at math, science, and engineering. Engineering is basically using math and science to build cool things, like computer guts.

I have spent so much time in these rooms because I've lived my whole life on the *Athena*. I'm a space kid! Space kids are what grown-ups call us kids who grow up in space. We don't live in houses with nice backyards. We can't even ride our bikes around the neighborhood like you land kids. Well, there was that one time Arnold rode down the hallway on a bike I built and almost crashed into Captain Jax, but I'll tell you about that some other time.

The *Athena* is a ship in AstroFleet, which is the science and defense force for the Planetary Republic. The Republic is a group of twenty planets that work together to make the galaxy a better place for all living things, even dentists (although I sent a letter to the president to get them taken off the list—I haven't heard back yet).

AstroFleet helps explore the galaxy and also defends the Planetary Republic from evil aliens. But it won't defend us from too much homework (although I sent a letter to the president to get homework added to the list of enemies, and this time they wrote back, "Please stop writing us."). At least after my homework is done, I can find some fun on the ship—like in these secret computer rooms.

I'm lucky Arnold and I are both smaller than other third graders, because my gut rooms are a little tight and stuffy. But I have had some really fun times behind the *Athena*'s walls doing things that usually get me sent to the brig.

Like this one time. . .

Oh, I'll tell you about that one another time. Back to this story for now.

We were still in the gut room near the bridge when Arnold looked through my backpack, took something out of it, and handed it to me.

"That's a Riglio B-52 digital splatz converter, not a screwdriver!" I said.

Sigh. Doesn't he know anything? Arnold may be my best friend, but sometimes I wish he knew lots about science and engineering, like I do. Oh well, we still have tons of fun together.

"Eudora, you said we would get to see the bridge's battle-training exercise," Arnold complained.

He does not always have the same thirst for adventure as I do.

Arnold wiped his wavy blond hair away from his eyes as he looked around some more in my backpack. He handed me a different tool.

I rolled my eyes at him. "That's a Bernetti X3 gravity wrench. Just get the tool with the purple handle." Purple is my favorite color.

He finally found it and handed it to me.

"Don't worry, we'll see the battle-training exercise," I said while I concentrated on the computer system. I started unscrewing a part of the computer panel. "I just need to make a few adjustments after I get this piece off."

"You said we would see it from the bridge, not from one of your dusty, little stomach caves," Arnold whined.

"Gut room, Arnold. I call them gut rooms. Guts, guts, guts!" I said, angrily. "And don't worry. We'll see it from the bridge," I continued, trying to calm down. "Trust me, I know what I'm doing." I took the computer panel off and looked inside.

"I could have just asked my dad to let us on the bridge," Arnold complained again. His forehead started to sweat. It was hot in the room.

"The battle exercise would be boring without these adjustments. You'll see," I replied. I found the part of the computer I needed and started typing in some computer code. "And you don't want to get your dad mixed up in this."

Arnold's dad is Lootenant (I'm not sure how to spell it, but this looks right) Londo. He's actually a big, strong alien called a Qlaxon. Londo is the chief of security and serves on the bridge of the *Athena*. Arnold is human though. Londo is really his stepdad. I'll explain it all later.

The bridge is where the senior officers run the ship and fight amazing space battles. It's the most exciting part of the entire ship, and kids usually never get to see the bridge. I want to be the chief engineer of an AstroLiner one day, but I would settle for captain. Either way, I want to be in the middle of the action.

"Oh no, this is another one of your crazy plans." Arnold sighed.

"Almost done," I replied as I made my final adjustment to the computer.

This morning in my cabin I created a small memory chip for my plan. Now I was installing it into the computer. Done.

"Okay, Arnold. Do you want to watch from the bridge or not? Let's go!" I got up and headed back to the air vent tunnel.

"Finally!" Arnold said.

Made in the USA
Middletown, DE
09 August 2021